It's Mountain Music to My Ears!

The Story of Billy Bob and the Appalachian Jamboree

By Rania

Copyright © 2022

No part of this book may be reproduced by any mechanical, photographic or electronic process, or in the form of the phonographic recording, nor may it be stored in a retrieval system, transmitted, or otherwise be copied for public or private use without written consent of the author.

This book is dedicated to Maggie Mae, a magnificent cat who lived a magical life in Mt. Hope, West Virginia.

Young Billy Bob was an Appalachian hare who hippity hopped without a care, although he sometimes stopped to breathe the fresh mountain air!

One evening, Billy Bob heard a strumming.
Strum, strum, strum.
It sounded like a fine tune. So he followed the sound through the holler, under the bright moon.
Until…he found…

A BIG BLACK BEAR!

The black bear's name was Jeb and he wore a fine ole' hat.
Jeb was strumming a tune on a banjo.
"A BANJO?" Billy Bob asked, "What's THAT?"
"Well, a banjo is a round instrument," Jeb said, "with five sturdy strings. You can pluck and strum it while you *sing*."

Jeb said the banjo came to Appalachia a long time ago, and mountain folks got to strumming and putting on musical shows.

But just then Billy Bob heard a different kind of strumming- a choppy, woody, fine little tune. So he said to Jeb, "I must go now but I'll be back soon!"

He hippity hopped through the woods until he found a silly opossum named Ned. And wouldn't you believe it? Ned was strumming an instrument just like Jeb!

But it wasn't a BANJO. It was shorter and had many more strings. It was a MANDOLIN that Ned was playing! And its sound went *tingity, twang, ting.*

But just then Billy Bob heard a *rake-ity*, rake tune. So he said to Ned, "I must go now but I'll be back soon!"

He hopped and hopped until he found…

Ray the Raccoon!

Ray was using his sharp claws to strum but with no chords.
This was because Ray was playing a simple washboard!

A WASHBOARD has a strong, hardy frame made of wood with metal parts you can rake to make music sound good. And it also can be used to scrub your clothes nice and clean. Take a good look and see what I mean!

"Here is a thimble, why don't you take a turn?" said Ray to Billy Bob who wanted to learn.

But as it turned out, playing the washboard would have to wait because Billy Bob heard *another* sound he had to investigate.

It was a *clickety*, clank tune.
So he said to Ray, "I must go now but I'll be back soon!"

The hare hippity hopped back down the holler, until he reached a stream. He heard an unlikely instrument. But it wasn't an instrument, or so it would seem…

He found Maggie Mae the Otter
slapping SPOONS upon her knee.
Spoons as musical instruments? he thought.
He was sure this couldn't be!

"You do not use these spoons to eat.
You clink and clank them to make a beat,"
said Maggie Mae with a smile so sweet.

But Billy Bob was looking elsewhere because he spotted a big fire burning in the air.
He listened a bit to Maggie Mae's spoon tune and then said to her, "I must go now but I'll be back soon!"

Billy Bob hippity hopped and hopped until he reached the mountaintop.

Just then, a squirrel named Bucky ran down. He was out of breath and spinning 'round and 'round. He carried a FIDDLE which is a folksy violin. Bucky loved to play the fiddle to entertain his kin.

He said, "Fire on the Mountain is what I call this fiery tune. I was playing so fast that I burned my cabin to ruins!"
But just then Billy Bob heard a noise- this time a sweet, old tune. So he said to Bucky, "I must go now but I'll be back soon!"

As Billy Bob turned around, he saw Darlene the Deer playing a pretty sound! "Hey y'all, come over here," she said. "I'm playing a mountain dulcimer, gather near."

A MOUNTAIN DULCIMER is like a banjo but it's not as round. It looks like a teardrop and makes a bright mountain sound.

By now, Billy Bob was awfully tired and knew he had to rest his head. So he hollered to his friends, "Let's make some mountain music and have a hoedown before bed!"

Printed in the USA
CPSIA information can be obtained
at www.ICGtesting.com
CBHW042333240824
13684CB00004B/15